I believe in you

WRITTEN AND ILLUSTRATED BY
Marianne Richmond

sourcebooks
jabberwocky

I believe in you

Published by Sourcebooks Jabberwocky, an imprint
of Sourcebooks, Inc.
P.O. Box 4410, Naperville, Illinois 60567-4410
(630) 961-3900
Fax: (630) 961-2168
www.jabberwockykids.com

Library of Congress Cataloging-in-Publication data
is on file with the publisher.

Source of Production: Leo Paper, Heshan City,
Guangdong Province, China.
Date of Production: April 2011
Run Number: 14999

Printed and bound in China.
LEO 10 9 8 7 6 5 4 3 2 1

**Also available from author & illustrator
Marianne Richmond:**

The Gift of an Angel
The Gift of a Memory
Hooray for You!
The Gifts of Being Grand
I Love You So…
Dear Daughter
Dear Son
Dear Granddaughter
Dear Grandson
Dear Mom
My Shoes Take Me Where I Want to Go
Fish Kisses and Gorilla Hugs
Happy Birthday to You!
I Love You So Much…
You Are My Wish Come True
Big Sister
Big Brother
If I Could Keep You Little
The Night Night Book
Beautiful Brown Eyes
Beautiful Blue Eyes
I Wished for You, an adoption story
I Believe in You
Daddy Loves Me!
Mama Loves Me!
Grandpa Loves Me!
Grandma Loves me!
Pink Wiggly Pig

Find more heartfelt books and
beautiful gifts for all occasions at
www.mariannerichmond.com

I believe in you

is dedicated to my four kids...
I will always be on your team!

You came into our family

with a **big, BIG** job to do,

the one of **growing up** into

**the one and
only you!**

Some days, it's **super easy.**

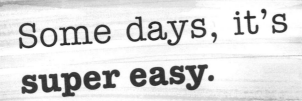

And others?
Kind of tough.

Monday's **"bring it on!"** turns into

Friday's **"had enough!"**

Whether it's **sunny** or stormy,

whether you're **happy** or blue,

I'm here to say,
without a doubt,

that **I believe in** *you!*

When your project
seems **too hard**,

and you want to go to bed,

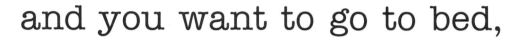

When the team you like says, "**No,**

some other kid
will play,"

I believe in your **awesome skills**

to shine another way.

When the monsters in your closet
seem **too big** for you to fight,

I believe in your
true courage

to know it'll
be **all right.**

When you make a **big mistake**

or you choose a
hurtful way,

I believe in your **stand-up truth**

to say
what **you**
should say.

When you look into the mirror

and question **who you see,**

I believe in
your **true beauty**

that shines through

from you to me.

When learning **something new**

makes you want
to stop and quit,

I believe in your **great attitude,** to go and conquer it!

Your job of *growing up*

takes
hard work,
I know,

but each
day is an
adventure.

Each
problem
helps you
grow.

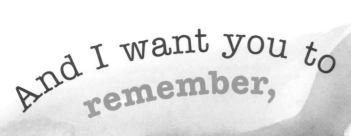

And I want you to remember,

I'm here to watch the ride.

I believe in one **amazing** *you*

with all my
love and pride!